The Very Wobbly Christmas

Written by
Sarah Naish & Rosie Jefferies

Illustrated by
Sarah Naish

Written for parents by Sarah Naish

The A-Z of Therapeutic Parenting- Strategies and Solutions- Jessica Kingsley Publishers 2018
But He Looks So Normal- CreateSpace/ Amazon 2016
Therapeutic Parenting in a Nutshell- Create Space/ Amazon 2016

Children's Books, written and illustrated by Sarah Naish available from Amazon and Amazon outlets

Teddy Tappy and the Tangley Memory Monster- A story about managing bad memories
ISBN-13: 978-1987553727

Children's Books, by Sarah Naish and Rosie Jefferies, available from Jessica Kingsley Publishing

William Wobbly and the Mysterious Holey Jumper -A story about fear and coping
Illustrated by Megan Evans ISBN 9781785922817 eISBN 9781784505868

Callum Kindly and the Very Weird Child A story about sharing your home with a new child Illustrated by
Megan Evans ISBN 9781785923005 eISBN 9781784506094

Rosie Rudey and the Enormous Chocolate Mountain -A story about hunger, overeating and using food for
comfort Illustrated by Megan Evans ISBN 9781785923029 eISBN 9781784506124

Katie Careful and the Very Sad Smile A story about anxious and clingy behaviour Illustrated by Megan Evans
ISBN 9781785923043 eISBN 9781784506100

William Wobbly and the Very Bad Day- A story about when feelings become too big
Illustrated by Amy Farrell ISBN 9781785921513 eISBN 9781784504113

Charley Chatty and the Wiggly Worry Worm A story about insecurity and attention-seeking Illustrated by
Amy Farrell ISBN 9781785921490 eISBN 9781784504106

Rosie Rudey and the Very Annoying Parent- A story about a prickly child who is scared of getting close
Illustrated by Amy Farrell ISBN 9781785921506 eISBN 9781784504120

Sophie Spikey Has a Very Big Problem -A story about refusing help and needing to be in control Illustrated by
Amy Farrell ISBN 9781785921414 eISBN 9781784504151

Charley Chatty and the Disappearing Pennies- A Story about stealing and lying.
Illustrated by Megan Evans ISBN 9781785923036 eISBN 9781784506117

Ellie Jelly and the Massive Mum Meltdown- A story about when parents lose their temper and need to put it
right. Illustrated by Kath Grimshaw ISBN9781785925160

Library of Congress Cataloguing in Publication Data A CIP catalogue record for this book is available from the Library of Congress British Library Cataloguing in Publication Data A CIP catalogue record for this book is available from the British Library
ISBN 978-1726626729

Mum needs to act fast to stop Christmas getting wobbly!

Everyone is getting more and more wobbly the closer Christmas gets! William Wobbly, Sophie Spikey, Charley Chatty, Rosie Rudey and Katie Careful are all trying their best but sometimes it's too difficult for them to stay calm.

In this story the children are all struggling with the changes which come with Christmas. Rosie wants to be in charge of everything, William is worried about Santa coming into the house, Sophie doesn't want to talk about anything, Charley is chatting even more than usual, and Katie just wants everything to go back to normal!

Luckily Mum has a plan to try to sort everything out and to make sure that this year is a bit easier than last Christmas.

Written by a Mum who helped her children sort out their Christmas wobbles, this story will help everyone to have a happier Christmas!

As soon as Hallowe'en was over, Rosie Rudey started being bossy about what she wanted for Christmas.

William Wobbly started feeling VERY Wobbly when he thought about Christmas.

Sophie Spikey became spikier, Katie Careful followed Mum about a bit closer and Charley Chatty chatted even more!

Mum did not think it was possible for Charley to chat more. But it was.

It sounded like the radio.

Mum noticed that all the children were more wobbly than usual, so she decided it was time to sort the wobbles out. She made 7 nice hot chocolates and called everyone into the kitchen for a 'big family chat.'

 Dad said he'd be 'back in a minute.'

The children and Mum all sat at the table. William had big saucer eyes because he was worried he might be in trouble.

Luckily Mum started off by saying, "Now, no one is in trouble, but I thought it was time to have a little chat about Christmas."

Straight away Rosie Rudey started speaking loudly in a rude voice saying what she wanted for Christmas and telling mum she had written a list.

Mum said, "It's not about the list or what you're having for Christmas. I have decided that we need to remember what happened last Christmas, so we can make sure that we have a nicer time this year."

Sophie Spikey said she had to go and do 'a very busy thing'.

Mum said that Sophie needed to stay at the table and drink her hot chocolate while they made plans together.

Sophie looked a bit spikey about that.

"Last year," Mum said, "I think things started to go wrong when I went to Charley's nativity play. I remember all the fairies coming out with their wings on, but when Charley was carried out by the teacher, she had a purple face and looked very angry about wearing her pink sparkly shoes.

"Charley, you were in a very bad mood after that. I know you have been worrying about the nativity play this year."

Charley said, "I'm not going to be a shepherd! I'm wearing my school uniform!"

Mum said, "That's fine then, this year you can wear your school uniform and I will tell the teacher that that is what is happening."

"Can I still sing 'the little bored Jesus' instead of 'the little lord Jesus?" Asked Charley.

"You can sing whatever you want as long as it's polite," Mum replied.

Mum explained, "I think everyone else struggled a bit as well when everything changed at school and there were suddenly lots of films to watch and plays to do. So, this year I'm speaking to the teacher about how we can keep things the same for everyone."

"Also, last Christmas I think things went wrong for William when the silly window cleaner told him that he had to be good because Santa would only bring presents for good children and then said Santa would be coming into our house."

William looked at the table and stared very hard, blinking his eyes and trying not to cry.

"Well I have written to Santa this year," continued Mum, "and I have received a reply to say that no matter what silly things anybody says to you, he is definitely coming to deliver the presents. I've sent him the key to the shed, so the presents will all be in there this year. Nobody is coming into the house. I will be locking the doors and Dad will double check."

"Santa said this was all fine and much quicker for him to do in any case."

"I remember that all those things made William so wobbly that he hid under the sideboard on Christmas Day and wouldn't come out to unwrap his presents until nearly lunchtime."

Then Mum explained, "This year we have decided that there will be a few presents in the morning a few at lunchtime, a couple at teatime and one just before bed. That way there will be no big pile to make everyone all panicky, wobbly and worried."

Rosie Rudey looked a bit cross about this and said, "I like having an enormous pile of presents! If everyone can't cope with it, I will just open everyone's for them!"

Mum said, "That won't be necessary Rosie, but thank you for your kind thoughts."

Mum remembered, "Last year you all got scooters because that's what you had all asked for. In fact, you asked for them lots and lots of times.....

.....My ears nearly fell off hearing about scooters."

All the children started feeling a bit itchy and squirmy when they remembered 'the scooter incident'.

"I know you have probably forgotten now," said Mum,
but by lunchtime on Christmas Day all the scooters were broken
after they had been thrown down the steps when you had a scooter
throwing competition. I think this happened because the wobbly part
of your brain was worried that you didn't deserve nice things and
needed to remind me that you still all feel wobbly inside, especially
at Christmas.

The children all concentrated hard on their hot chocolates.

"Well this year I have decided that whatever you get will be chosen especially for you by me and will be the right thing for you. We will not be looking at lots of lists of presents or concentrating on one very important present."

Charley said, "Well it was Katie who threw my scooter down the steps...

...I didn't even do anything!"

Katie looked a bit sad.

Mum said it was very sad that the scooters had been broken but that no blaming or arguing was necessary as she would be more careful this year and help everyone not to break things.

Sophie Spikey whispered to Katie that Christmas had only been horrible because Rosie had eaten all the advent calendar chocolates and then stolen all the selection boxes too. Luckily, just before Katie started doing angry blaming and shouting, Mum said, "I heard what you said Sophie, I think you meant to make Rosie and Katie have a little fight then."

Sophie went all blotchy and hot.

"Anyway," said Mum, "this year I will be using an advent calendar that Granny made with lots of pockets in."

"I will be putting in 5 sweets at breakfast time for you all to have one each before school.

There won't be any in any of the other days just in case people want to do extra sharing with themselves."

Most of the children stared at their hot chocolates.

Rosie stared at her empty cup.

"There's just one more change," Mum said, "this year we won't be doing any visiting. We are having a quiet time at home with a lovely dinner and lots of time to play with your presents.

"Dinner will be at the usual time, but you can all go to bed one hour later."

Just then, Dad wandered in hoping that the serious talk was over now.

Luckily it was.

Katie Careful felt a happy bubble feeling in her tummy about not having to go visiting.

Last year she remembered she had felt very wobbly when Uncle John said she was naughty because she couldn't sit still at the table.

There had been lots of pointy eyebrows on the grown ups' faces and Rosie had thrown her empty plate on the floor!

Charley Chatty was very pleased when she wore her school uniform at the Nativity. All the parents made sad faces at her and asked if she had forgotten her costume.

Mum said, "No, Charley is wearing what she wants to. I am so pleased that she is an individual."

On Christmas Eve, William helped Dad to unlock the shed and make room for the presents Santa was bringing.

William was VERY happy Santa wasn't coming into the house, even if he WAS kind and magic!

That Christmas, all the children were much less wobbly.

Mum said she had had 'quite a nice time,' even though there had been some arguing about who had the best presents.

Dad said he had had a 'MUCH better time this year,' as he hadn't spent all day trying to fix broken scooters.

The children all said it had been 'the BEST CHRISTMAS EVER!'

.....But to be fair they did say that every year!

L-R Sophie Spikey, Katie Careful, Charley Chatty, William Wobbly and Rosie Rudey on Christmas Day (before 'the scooter incident').

L-R Katie Careful, William Wobbly, Charley Chatty, Sophie Spikey and Rosie Rudey- Christmas Day.

The End

A note for parents and carers, from the authors

This book was written to help you to help your children. All the children in the stories are based on real children and life events.

This Christmas story names feelings for the child, and also gives parents and carers therapeutic parenting strategies to manage feelings of anxiety which seem to arise at this time of year. It brings together all five children from our family and explores common issues we encountered.

Therapeutic parents, (such as adopters and foster carers), often tell us that they feel out of their depth, and don't know what to say or do when faced with the behaviours we encounter. This story not only gives you valuable insight into WHY our children behave this way, but also enables you to read helpful words, through a third party therapeutic parent, to your child to explain the feelings and resulting behaviours to them.

Consistency- Therapeutic parents need to keep strong routine and boundaries. This can be a challenge at Christmas time when routines slip. School in particular, may pose challenges around changes in routine with unrealistic expectations around this. Here, the parent confronts this head on and states what is changing, identifying that this might make the children feel 'more wobbly'. This enables our children to understand that this is not their fault, but something commonly experienced by children who have suffered trauma.

Visiting and managing the expectations of others – There is often pressure on us as parents to make Christmas even more difficult by visiting relatives who may not understand our children's need for structure and routine at Christmas time. This can lead to us having a very fraught time! Think carefully about what is and is not manageable for your children. A quiet Christmas Day at home may well be a much easier day for everyone!

Sabotage – We see in this story how the children have destroyed a present, despite appearing to be very keen on receiving them! This happens when there is a conflict with the child's internal working model. (sense of self) and the parents projection of that. I.e. if a child feels they are 'bad', when we give them something nice they may feel compelled to ruin the moment and remind us 'who they are'.

Empathy and nurture – Throughout the story the parent is present and offering nurture and empathy. The hot chocolates represent the nurture! The parent empathises with each child's previously experienced difficulties at the last Christmas without blame and recrimination.

Christmas preparation – It is worthwhile giving some serious thought to preparing your children regarding popular fables. What does it mean to them if a strange man comes into the house at night when they are sleeping? Even if it is Santa! Is this something they can manage? At the same time, you need to give your children a clear message about the link between 'being good' and Santa visiting/ not visiting. Well-meaning adults may tell your children they must be good, or he will not come, but this can catapult our children into sabotaging behaviour.

Sarah is a therapeutic parent of five adopted siblings, now all adults, CEO of the National Association of Therapeutic Parents, (www.naotp.com), former social worker and previous owner of an 'Outstanding' therapeutic fostering agency. Rosie, her daughter, checked and amended the children's thoughts and expressed feelings to ensure they are as accurate a reflection as possible.

Together, Rosie and Sarah now spend all their time working within the NATP, and delivering training and conferences through Fostering Attachments Ltd, (Inspire Training Group), helping parents, carers, social workers and other professionals to heal traumatised children, nationally and internationally. www.inspiretraininggroup.com

You can also find more help at The National Association of Therapeutic Parents.

Please use this story to make connections, explain behaviours, and build attachments between your child and yourself.

Therapeutic Parenting makes everything possible.

Warmest Regards,

Sarah Naish & Rosie Jefferies

Made in the USA
Monee, IL
23 November 2020